Charles Lewis Bartholomew

Cartoons of the Spanish-American War

Charles Lewis Bartholomew

Cartoons of the Spanish-American War

ISBN/EAN: 9783741191596

Manufactured in Europe, USA, Canada, Australia, Japa

Cover: Foto ©Andreas Hilbeck / pixelio.de

Manufactured and distributed by brebook publishing software
(www.brebook.com)

Charles Lewis Bartholomew

Cartoons of the Spanish-American War

Cartoons

Of the

Spanish-American War

By Bart

With Dates of

Important Events

From The

Minneapolis Journal

January

1899

Preface

• • •

THE picture language was the earliest form of written expression. It is still under some conditions the most effective. The cartoonist often hits the bull's eye harder and makes the bell ring louder than the writer of the most vigorous and forcible English.

Among cartoonists, none excell "Bart," whose clever and intelligent pencil is doing the most effective work in that line to be found in any American newspaper. When, a few weeks ago, a publishing house in Chicago issued a large book containing five hundred and fifty of the best cartoons of the war from twelve foreign and twenty-nine American journals,—the leading English, American, French, German, Spanish and Mexican papers—it was found that the publishers had selected twice as many of "Bart's" cartoons as of any other cartoonist.

The picture history of the war has been written in the Journal more fully than in any other paper, no opportunity being lost to present the important war events of the day from the cartoon standpoint. These cartoons are reproduced here, and it is believed they will be found a valuable and interesting part of the story of an eventful year.

THE JOURNAL.

MERELY A FRIENDLY OALL.

January 24, 1898.

January 26, 1898, found the battle-ship Maine on a friendly mission to Havana. This was the beginning of the end. Spain never considered this "a friendly call." On February 15th, the Maine was destroyed by the explosion of a sub-marine mine. Whatever historians may decide was the cause of the war, the destruction of the Maine certainly was the crisis that precipitated it. This

HOT STUFF.

The Kentucky May Be Christened With Water, But When She Goes to Sea She Will Be Loaded Like This.—January 28

terrible catastrophe, with the death of 260 American sailors, followed by Captain Sigbee's admonition to the people of the United States to "suspend judgment" called out very few, if any, cartoons on the event itself. It was too ghastly a thing to picture– an act of war in a time of peace. The

THE SENATE'S SIAMESE TWINS.

That Body Would Force Mr. McKinley to Take Both or Neither.—February 3.

cartoonists trained their guns on the offender later. The islands of Cuba and Hawaii solicited the attention of the President and the people of the United States, bound together. The question of the annexation of Hawaii was before congress, together with the recognition of Cuba, before the Maine crisis brought us face to face with war. After war was begun, Hawaii became a military necessity and so a part of the United States. The needs of the two peoples started us expanding.

LITTLE DUPUY DE LOME'S OOMIC VALENTINE.

February 10.

Five days before the Maine was blown up, the real Spanish feeling bubbled over at Washington in an utterance of their minister to this country who referred to President McKinley as a pot-hunting

WILL IT COME TO THIS?
February 19.

politician. A few days sufficed to satisfy the people of this country that Spain, or some of her officials, was guilty of the Maine horror. Indignation knew no bounds. Retaliation was demanded. The necessary delay for official investigation irritated the people and made this cartoon (Feb'y 19) the most popular of the week. Subsequent events have vindicated President McKinley's

A SUSPICIOUS LOOKING FISH.

While Uncle Sam Has His Diving Clothes on He Might Do a Thorough Job of This Investigation in Cuban Waters.—February [illegible]

course. Official investigation began at once. It was plain that the monster guilty of sinking the Maine must be brought to account for other and more terrible misdeeds. Spain claimed, of course,

IS THIS AN ACCIDENT?

February 21.

that the explosion that destroyed the Maine, whether internal or external, was accidental. A glance over her record in Cuba showed that there was much of this sort of thing that could hardly be an

WAR HAS BEEN DEOLARED.

The Fearless Yellow Journals Open Up Operations on the Enemy. February 23.

accident. While the President and the business interests of the country were doing their utmost to avert the horrors of war, if the same end could be accomplished by peaceful means, the sensational newspapers of the country began operations. A period of waiting followed during which

PEACEFUL ON THE SURFACE—BUT ?

March 1.

every effort was made to preserve peace, but no time or opportunity was lost to prepare for war. Whether we fought Spain or not, there was no longer any question as to our duty to starving Cuba.

LET THIS WAR GO ON.

March 3.

and the country said "Let This War Go On," when Uncle Sam started his war ships towards Cuba with fifty tons of food. By the first of March war was a foregone conclusion and was the topic of

THIS WILL SETTLE IT.

The American Wheelman Will Join in the War on Spain—Poor Spain!—March 1.

main interest in congress and out. Nothing else could be heard. Congress furnished President McKinley with $50,000,000 to spend in preparing for the impending conflict. There was no lagging

SOME GOOD FROM IT.

Those Dogs Do Make a Terrible Noise, to Be Sure, But They Have Drowned Out the Wail of the Calamity Howler.—March 5.

but all parties kept step to the President's music in the most patriotic fashion. Two cartoons, "The First Gun," and "They Keep Step," published respectively March 8 and March 9, were

THE FIRST GUN.
Congress Heard From. March 8

especially popular, being reproduced in The Review of Reviews, Literary Digest, Detroit Tribune St. Louis Globe-Democrat, and other publications. Gopher hearts beat fast when, on March 10, the

THEY KEEP STEP.

March 9.

good ship Minneapolis, the fastest cruiser in the navy, was ordered to the front to be ready for action. England early took opportunity to commend the action of the United States in its dealings with Spain.

MINNEAPOLIS TO THE FRONT.
March 10

We were, perhaps, a little slow to recognize the advantage of this. The Review of Reviews, in commenting on the John Bull cartoon, March 11, said that all that was asked of England was to remain

GREAT HEAD JOHN BULL.

J. Bull—'Il There, Brother Jonathan. Hi'll 'Elp You Lick Yer' Man, Hand You 'Elp Me Wallop Them Saucy Cusses on the 'Uother Side the Fence. We Can Lick the Whole Bloomin' Houtfit, Me 'Earty, Don't Cher Know!—March 11.

neutral. The official report from the board of inquiry into the Maine disaster was anxiously awaited. The country knew this report must be a war-like one, but the signal must come before war began

REPORT OF THE MAINE BOARD OF INQUIRY.

That Is What Uncle Sam Is Listening for So Anxiously.—March 11.

The President was not many days in making use of part of that $50,000,000, and by the middle of March had purchased two ships of Brazil. Spain was looking at bargains in this line but had no

DOGS OF WAR.

Alfonso: Bow-Wow! Bow-Wow!! Bow-Wow!!! My Warships Can't Buy Me a Bow-Wow! March 15

money or credit. Minnesota's representatives in congress had their share in the moulding of events in our foreign relations. Congressman Tawney visited Hawaii in the interest of the United States,

BRINGING IT HOME TO US.

Senator Davis—Say Jim, If Uncle Sam Doesn't Want This Thing We'll Just Put It in the Upper Lake at Minnetonka and Annex It to Minnesota. March 17.

---

and Senator Davis, as chairman of the foreign relations committee, was a leading spirit throughout the war. The condition of the reconcentrados in Cuba grew worse, if such a thing were possible,

COLUMBUS AGAIN BEFORE THE SPANISH THRONE.

Alfonso (sadly)—O Chris! Why Did You Ever Discover Those Troublesome Americans?—March 21.

during the time the United States menaced Spain with war. Men like Senator Proctor personally investigated their condition and reported it worse than had been pictured by newspaper correspond-

IF THIS IS INTERVENTION LET U. S. INTERVENE.

Uncle Sam to Spain—I Propose to Feed Starving Cuba—With Your Consent If You Please, Without It If You Don't! See?—March 12.

---

ents. Spain stood persistently in the way of all relief expeditions. The war comet was close upon us, and quite as apparent to the observer as Perrine's during the last week in March. Uncle Sam's

HEADED THIS WAY.

Perrine's Is Not the Only Comet in the Sky. Uncle Sam's May Not Be Coming at the Rate of a Million Miles a Day, But It Is Coming Fast Enough. March [illegible]

---

beautiful white war ships were cleared for action and painted an ugly lead color so they would not be so readily seen by the enemy or prove so good a mark. The navy officials did not know then

UNOLE SAM PUTS ON WAR PAINT.

March 29.

that the Spanish gunners could not hit them anyway. The ships of Spain were at this time reported to be painted black and ready for war. The war fever ran high on March 29. The report

TIME TO "TAKE THE BULL BY THE HORNS."

March 29.

---

of the board of inquiry was expected at any time, and the public knew pretty well what it would be. War resolutions were introduced in congress and thrilling speeches made. The country was satisfied it was time to take the Spanish bull by the horns. The attitude of congress now became

ANOTHER MINE.

Prest. McKinley—I Wonder If That Thing Will Go Off?—March 30

threatening. Tom Reed lost his upper hand in the house and the prospect was good that President McKinley's hand would be forced. President McKinley had been credited with having a well de-

HOLDING THE WATCH ON HIM.

Uncle Sam—You'll Have to Shoot Pretty Quick Mac, or We'll Conclude the Old Thing Isn't Loaded. March 31

lined policy in regard to Cuba and Spain, but the country began, at this time, to doubt it. Perhaps the President was only waiting until he could see the "whites of the enemy's eyes." Sagasta, on

The Eagle—Oh, We're Onto You, Sagasta; This is April 1.—April 1.

the first of April, came forward with new proposals as to how the difficulty might be settled. It was, of course, the part of the diplomat playing for more time, and quite in line with the spirit of the day. The President declined the spurious sweets. The question of what the powers of Europe

SAGASTA PLAYS FOR EUROPEAN SYMPATHY.

But There Doesn't Seem to Be Much Chance of His Getting the Bouquet.—April 2.

would do about it excited much interest. France, Austria and Germany were unquestionably friendly to Spain, but the official bouquet of sympathy was never let fall. The dilatory tactics of

OFF COMES HIS COAT--NOW LOOK OUT!

April 4.

Sagasta made Uncle Sam peel off his coat and stand waiting for the word from the President and congress to give Spain the thrashing he so richly deserved. Even at this early stage, before war

NO ROOM FOR HIM ON THIS SIDE.
April 5.

had been declared, it was plain that when the patient boot of Uncle Sam was lifted to kick against Spain's atrocities in Cuba, it would result in the tyrant being driven from the western hemisphere.

THE SPANISH CAVALIER--UP TO DATE.

A Spanish Cavalier Stood in His Retreat, The Music So Sweet, Did Oft Times Repeat,
And On His Guitar Played a Tune, Dear; Remember What He says Isn't True Dear.—April 7.

Sagasta's guitar of diplomacy twanged loudly in these days for delay, but the music was discord to the American ear. For days in succession the President's message to congress, declaring for war.

ONLY A QUESTION OF TIME.

Uncle Sam: It's Always, Tomorrow, Tomorrow, Tomorrow; but if Tomorrow Ever Comes I'll Knock That Fellow Into the Middle of Next Week.—April 5.

was promised to come on the following day. Uncle Sam grew very impatient. Preparations for

AN EXPECTED TESTIMONIAL.

Dear Uncle Sam: I Have Used Your Quick Rising Powder and Will Have Occasion to Use No Other, I Think, for Some Time.
April 11. Yours Truly, Spain.

---

war, which had been carried on in secret all this time, now came to the surface in an order by the United States for $15,000,000 worth of red prismatic powder. Poor old Uucle Sam, never before in

OVERWORKED.

Uncle Sam to the Cartoonists of the Country—Don't You Think, Boys, You Could Give Me a Day Off? I Begin to Feel as if I Had Been Worked Overtime by You Fellows of Late.—April 9.

his career had been in such demand by the cartoonists of the country. It really developed the war-

IT TAKES TWO TO GET PEACE OUT OF AN ARMISTICE.

April 12.

---

like Uncle Sam. The plan of autonomy adopted by Spain, at the last moment, in Cuba began to show itself a dismal failure, for one reason, because it takes two to get peace out of an armistice.

ABOUT MOVING TIME.

Spain—Wouldn't Wonder If It May Be Necessary for Me to Go Before "Moving Day." This Place Is Very Unhealthy.—April 13.

It was indeed moving time for Spain in Cuba. On April 11, the President announced to congress that his best endeavors for a peaceful solution of the trouble had failed, and asked that body to empower him to use the army and navy of the United States to stop the war, and to continue generous

REED'S REOONOENTRADOS BROKE LOOSE YESTERDAY.

A Suggestion as to How They Might Better Have Used Their Ammunition Instead of Wasting it on One Another.—April 11.

relief to the starving people of Cuba. Now that congress had the matter in their own hands, for several days they did more fighting among themselves than against Cuba. Ink wells proved good missiles, and a free fight for free Cuba came off among Tom Reed's reconcentrados on the 13th.

NOT THIS—BUT
RECOGNITION NOT DEMANDED.
THIS!
April 15.

BLOWING UP SPAIN.

If Talking Could Settle It, Our Senate Would Make Short Work of This War.—April 16.

The dignified senate followed the example of the house, and wasted much breath which was not all directed against Spain. The question of paying for the luxury arose before war began, and when the

WAR TAOKS VS. PATRIOTISM.

This Patriot Was Whooping For War Until He Came In Contact With the War Tacks.—April 18.

war tax was put into operation it reached every patriot who had been so long calling for war. The

THOSE GOVERNMENT MULES.

A Week of This Kind of Progress Made the Country Tired, but Uncle Sam Finally Got the Mastery.—April 18.

house and senate spent nine days getting those war resolutions into action, and then, by a vote of 42 to 35 in the senate and 311 to 6 in the house, they resolved: That the people of the island of Cuba are, and

MAKE HIM WALK SPAMSH.

Uncle Sam—Now Git—Durn Ye! · April 20.

of right ought to be, free, and independent, and furthermore demand that Spain get out of Cuba. The next day the President signed this document, and a copy was sent to the Spanish minister who decided he must go home. He was not the only one to "walk Spanish" during the season. The Span-

MAKING A FOURTH OF JULY FOR CUBA.

April 21.

---

ish minister failed to communicate this little note to his home government, and the next day the President wired the ultimatum to our minister in Spain giving the Don until noon of the 23d to reply. But Spain didn't want to recognize this note, so told Gen. Woodford that they considered the Presi

A CORKER FOR SPAIN.
April 22

dent's approval of the joint resolution as equivalent to an actual declaration of war. Thus Spain started the ball rolling. On April 22 the Cuban ports were blockaded, and on that same date the Journal ran the cartoon "A Corker for Spain." On no other subject did the cartoonists get together

HAVANA FILLER.

How Uncle Sam Will Smoke the Spanish Out.—April 23.

as on this one of bottling up the enemy. Even the Spanish artists had Schley, Sampson and Dewey bottled up by their antagonists. The Journal was the first in the field with a bottling cartoon. It was supposed that Havana would be bombarded at the beginning of the war. No one dreamed

JOHNNY GET YOUR GUN.

April 25.

at this time of the island being surrendered without an attack on Havana being necessary. From the time of the blockade being declared the news of the bombardment of Havana was daily expected. President McKinley made his first call for volunteers on April 23. He asked for 125,000

MAKES NO DIFFERENCE TO HIM.

General Ramon Blanco (of Havana)—What's This, Wheat Is Up to $1.20 at Minneapolis—Well, I'll Not Take Any To-day.—April 25

men. If the number had been double that there would have been good men enough and to spare. As it was there were not guns for all the hands that reached for them. Wheat took a boom on the war and went up to $1.20 at Minneapolis. Gen. Blanco and the other inhabitants of Havana were

POOR OLD SPAIN.

Old Mother Hubbard
Went to the Cupboard
To Get Her Poor Dog a Bone—
When She Got There
The Cupboard was Bare
And So the Poor Dog Got None.—April 27.

---

unaffected by this rise in price of a main commodity, though they were already short of food. All supplies were shut off from them by the blockading squadron. Sagasta's war dog went hungry from the first. The American congress placed a $50,000,000 bone before our healthy dog of war and

PROSPEOTS FOR A SHOWER.

The Rainy Season Is At Hand in Cuba, and Somebody's Going to Get Wet.—April 28.

he was strong for the fray. Spain had no such offering. The rainy season was now at hand in Cuba and it did rain pitchforks for the Spanish occupants of the island. On the whole, however, it

THE DAY THE EAGLE SCREAMS.

April 29.

---

proved a refreshing shower, much needed to clear the Cuban atmosphere. On April 29, the Minnesota boys went into camp to await the orders of the President. It was a glorious day in the Twin Cities, and the way the eagle screamed will long be remembered. On Sunday, May 1, Dewey

UNCLE SAM--REMEMBER THE MAINE?

May 3.

destroyed the Spanish fleet at Manilla and it was pertinent for Uncle Sam, viewing the wreck of the Spanish ships, to inquire of Spain "Remember the Maine?" Butcher Weyler's type-writer

IF WEYLER IS COMING.

Uncle Sam Should Enlist the Typewriter Girls and Be Ready to Meet the Foreign Invader With His Own Kind of Weapons.—May 4.

got a going back in Spain now, and promised dreadful things for the United States in the way of an invasion headed by this gentleman. It seemed Uncle Sam might need a new kind of army for

AN INTERNAL EXPLOSION NEXT.

It Will Require No Court of Inquiry to Determine What Wrecked the Old Spanish Ship of State.—May 5.

such a foe. Don Carlos and the friends of the pretender in Spain promised disaster for the little king and the helmsman who was running the Spanish ship of state over the troubled seas of these

WILL WEAR THE STARS AND STRIPES.

Uncle Sam—Here Sonny, Put on These Duds.—May 7.

times. Porto Rico, the out-post of all the Antilles was a vantage point of much value. Uncle Sam kept his eye on this sentinel and it was early understood that when Spain was driven from the western hemisphere, Porto Rico would wear the stars and stripes. Porto Rico seemed willing.

The Kind of a Campaign Uncle Sam is Expected to Make and Make it Quick, Too.—May 9.

As for Cuba, it was all along a case of carrying bread on the bayonet to the starving. Cervera's

WILL SMITE THEM HIP AND THIGH.

Strong Man Sampson, of the U. S. Navy—Where Are the Blamin' Philistines?—May 10.

fleet was on its way to Cuba, and Sampson was after him to crush his force if possible on the high seas. But the ocean is wide, and this was the beginning of a long search and much guarding and

LANDING ON CUBA.
May 12.

anxiety along the American coast. Small detachments of United States troops were landed along the coast of Cuba at this time to co-operate with the insurgents and make ready for a land cam-

UNCLE SAM, AS THE STRONG MAN, SURPRISES THE SPECTATORS AT THE SHOW.

May 13.

---

paign against Havana. The Manilla incident together with the spirited manner in which Uncle Sam was doing his work on this side of the ocean caused much comment from the European press which, as a whole, expressed surprise at the strength Uncle Sam displayed. Sampson found time

NO, NEVER TOUCHED THEM!

May 14.

to slip into Porto Rico and drop a few shells about the head of Governor-General Macias. That gentleman, with true Spanish unveracity, reported to Madrid, "Never Touched Us." The people

THE JACK THAT OOULD TAKE SAGASTA'S LITTLE KING AND THE GAME.
May 16.

of Spain were very much dissatisfied with this one-sided war. Mobs flourished, news of disasters were kept from the people through press censorship. It seemed the people of Spain were more than ready to take Sagasta's little king and the game with the Carlos' jack. Cabinets went to pieces

POOR MATERIAL FOR A NEW CABINET.

May 17.

very easily in Spain, and it was difficult for Sagasta to find good material for new ones. It was evident to the Spaniards that they would only get blame and dishonor for serving in the cabinet at

BETTER FRIENDS THAN THEY USED TO BE.

May 18.

this time. The English Lion was very good to us in these days, and the Eagle smiled back his

OUR NEW NAVAL POLICY—GIVING 'EM MORE ROPE.

May 19.

---

appreciation. Schley and Sampson were given more freedom in their search for the wily Cervera. It was a noticeable fact that American admirals did better when farthest from Washington in-

UNCLE SAM AS A DISCOVERER.

Columbus—Hello There, Old Man—You Seem to Be Having About as Hard a Time Discovering the Spanish as I Had Discovering You.—May 20.

structions. Cervera had slipped by the American searchers, and the shade of Columbus was quite justified in his josh at Uncle Sam's expense. On May 20 came the report that the foxy Cervera was

GOT HIM TREED?

May 21.

cornered at last at Santiago. Before this cartoon got into the paper it was found necessary to run a question mark after it. Several days elapsed before it was certain that Cervera was up the tree.

HOW TIMES HAVE CHANGED.

The War Rumor to the Klondike Rumor—Here, You old Whiskers, Get Off the Earth. You're not in It With Me.—May 23.

Rumors flew thick and fast, but they were all war rumors. ‘-Kloudyke gold, which had been the main topic of interest, now had to give way to glory and the war rumor. There was much

While the French Are Talking of an Alliance With Spain, It May Be Well for Them to Remember the Mane.—May 21.

published relative to France giving Spain aid in the struggle. France probably never contemplated antagonizing the United States, but her actions at home gave rise to rumors not calculated to increase the friendship between the two republics. France had troubles of her own with the English Lion and she probably did remember the "Mane." Schley was left to watch

SPAIN IN THE HOLE.

May 29.

the entrance to Santiago harbor where Cervera disappeared. The public watched this game of cat and mouse with interest for days. The question arose, "How does our commander pronounce his name?" and after it was all over, it was decided that, before the night of July 3, it was pronounced "Sly," and afterward, "Slay."

SHAKE WELL BEFORE TAKING.

May 27.

The Spanish fleet was in fact bottled up securely, and the manner in which the American shells were dropped over the hills into Santiago harbor suggested that Schley might shake the Spanish well before taking. The great American eagle was now about ready to call in

OLUOK! OLUOK!! OLUOK!!

May 28.

the brood of little eaglets. Dewey had captured the Philippines. Hawaii was soon to come in through act of congress. Cuba was surrounded and about to fall, and Sampson was after Porto Rico. This was indeed a great Memorial Day. The brave boys who were taking

THE BOYS OF '76 AND '61 PASS ON "OLD GLORY" TO THE BOYS OF '98.
May 20.

up the colors that had never known defeat were, many of them, to fall within five weeks, before Santiago. Christian crusader never died in a more glorious cause. They died as Columbia's sons have always died, for freedom's cause. The Spanish fighter was now having an unpleasant time in

A PRECARIOUS POSITION.

May 31

the ring he had chosen. On May 30, Commodore Schley's squadron bombarded the forts guarding the mouth of Santiago harbor. It takes none of the glory from the seven brave men who went out

WHAT OUR NAVY IS MADE OF.

Four Hundred Men Volunteered When Sampson Asked for Men to Take the Merrimac Into the Mouth of Santiago Harbor, at the Risk of Almost Certain Death.—June 4.

---

to meet death with Lieut. Hobson to recall that four hundred men offered themselves to go on the expedition to block Santiago harbor by sinking the collier Merrimac into its narrow outlet.

THE EAGLE PULLS A FEW.

Spanish Honor May Thus Be Vindicated, but the Vain Bird Will Have Little Left of Which to Be Proud.—June 7.

The unequal struggle between the Eagle and the Peacock was beginning to tell on the beauty of the haughty bird. The colonial possessions of Spain at one time made a gorgeous display. It was left to the Eagle to pluck the few remaining feathers. The War Revenue act of June 13, levied heavily

TWO PATRIOTS.

Herr Beer to Col. Tobacco—Well, Old Man, We Won't Go Back on Uncle Sam in an Emergency Like This, Will We?—June 5.

on our two "patriots" here, beer and tobacco. They seemed to thrive under the tax, however. This act also authorized a 3 per cent. popular loan not to exceed $400,000,000. Of this, $200,000,000 was

WILL THE BIG SENTINEL LET HIM SLIP IN AT LAST?

June 10.

offered at once and "went like hot cakes." With the passport—"A Military Necessity"—Hawaii slipped into the United States' stockade. This cartoon, published June 10, preceded the big vote in the house in favor of annexation, which came on June 15, and stood 209 to 91 in favor of annexation

BOTH DOGS LOOSE NOW.

June 13.

While Cervera was at large, no attempt was made to start the troops to Cuba, but the army was cut loose to help the navy as soon as possible after this menace was removed. Six hundred marines landed in Guantanamo bay on June 10 and held their position. This was the first landing of an organized force. On June 22, Gen. Shafter landed at Daiquiri with the invading army. On June 23, the movement against Santiago was begun. On June 24, the first serious engagement took

THE FLYING SQUADRON HAS ITS EYE ON THE CANARIES.

June 20.

place. The Atlantic coast cities of the United States had their time of uneasiness when Cervera's fleet was at large. The fact that our flying squadron did not visit the coast of Spain, or at least pounce down upon the Canaries, was doubtless a surprise as well as a relief to the Spanish. From the very first of the war this expedition to the Canary islands was talked of as our next move, but

"CARRYING THE WAR INTO AFRICA."

"The Yankee Pig" Will Soon Be Rooting Things Up Along the Shores of Old Spain. June 23.

---

it never came. Admiral Camara, with Spain's Mediterranean fleet, started through the Suez canal to relieve Manilla. This started the talk of an American squadron to go to Spain and menace

THERE'S AN AFRICAN ON THE COAL PILE.

June 20.

---

that coast. Spain became very uneasy and Camara returned. You could almost smell the powder in the air on the Saturday preceding the Fourth of July. The Journal had good reason to

HURRAH FOR THE FOURTH OF JULY.

We're Coming In on Independence Day Celebrations, Too.—July 2.

make the cartoon of Hawaii, Cuba and the Philippines coming in for an independence day celebration. For two days we had had reports of furious fighting before Santiago. It was a Fourth

UNCLE SAM'S STRING OF CANNON CRACKERS.

July 4.

---

of July year for Cuba indeed. The sun rose on Cervera's fleet destroyed. The Spanish admiral could not have planned a more glorious Fourth for the United States. The string of cannon crackers

AFTER THE FOURTH.

Alphonso XIII—Well, I've Had Enough of These American Fireworks.—July 5.

started with a boom. The little Spanish King had indeed had enough of the American Fourth and American fireworks. The day saw their fleet destroyed, their army routed and left them without any hope of contesting further the American arms. Blanco sent false dispatches to Spain as to the

POOR, OLD SPAIN.

Blinded and Led Astray by Those in Whom It Has Placed Its Trust. It Is on the Brink of Ruin.—July 4.

battle, and the Spanish newspapers aided in deluding the people for days as to the result. Sagasta, perhaps afraid to interfere with the public will, allowed things to take their course. Old Spain was indeed blinded and lead astray by false guides, but he was happy in his ignorance. France

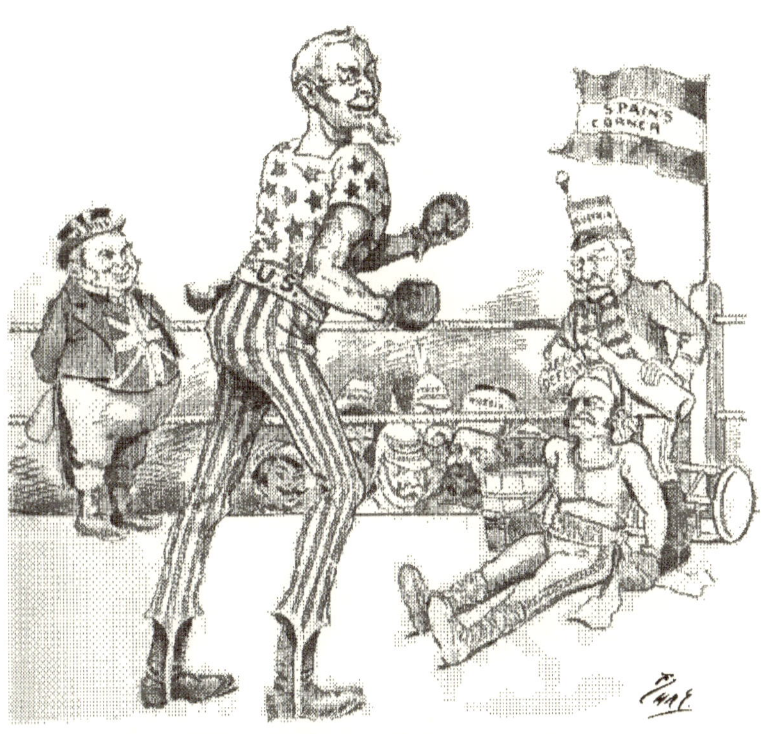

DOES NOT KNOW WHEN HE'S WHIPPED.

Voices From the Ring Side—Better Throw Up the Sponge, Don. You're Done For. July 7.

---

and other friendly advisors began at once to try to break it gently to Spain that he was whipped. Gen. Linares was still holding out at Santiago in spite of the protestations of the foreign consuls.

WEIGHING THE BABY.

July 8.

The Hawaiian resolution passed the senate on July 7, by a vote of 42 to 21, and Uncle Sam weighed the new baby with evident signs of satisfaction at what the scales read. The only thing in sight

OUT THEY GO--BACK THEY COME!

The Little King of Spain "Makes Believe" War With Camara's Fleet and Keeps a String To It. July 7.

for the American navy to fight now was Camara's fleet, and at this time it seemed certain Watson would go after them. Camara's movements, or reported movements, were as uncertain as though

THE LITTLE KING OF SPAIN AND THE YANKEE PIG.

As He Dreamed It Would Be—and—As It Is.—July 12.

the little King were playing with his ships. The Spaniards had so much fun out of the Yankee pig that the American cartoonists had to get even by putting their version of the Yankee pig on

UNCLE SAM'S ARITHMETIC CLASS.

Uncle Sam to Alfonso XIII.—There Now, Do You Think You Can Remember the Maine?--July 13

for a few evenings in this country. It was also fitting to strike a balance between the cost to Spain, and the cost to the United States in destroyed war ships. Yes, Spain could probably, now,

UNCLE SAM SWINGS HIS HAMMOCK.

The Conditions in Cuba Have Been Slightly Changed in the Last Few Days.—July 15.

"Remember the Maine." On July 15, Uncle Sam swung his hammock in Santiago, which surrendered without the bombardment which had been promised nearly every day since the Fourth. About

SIGNS OF PEACE.

July [illegible].

July 16, Uncle Sam, the Noah on the war flood, welcomed in a dove with a small olive branch and some peace talk from Spain. This was Spain's first sign of weakening. Other countries had predicted it since the Fourth, but it took Spain some time to come to it. July 18th it was given out

IN OLD SPAIN.

They Will Soon Be "Gathering Up the Shells by the Sea Shore"—July 18.

that Watson would start for the coast of Spain that same week with a formidable fleet. It seemed likely patrons of fashionable seaside resorts might soon be picking up the shells by the seashore.

NEXT.

July 19.

And now that Santiago had a hair cut and close shave, and the Philippine gentleman was cared for, Uncle Sam turned to Porto Rico and remarked that he was Next! Sanitary reforms were at

IT'S DIFFERENT UNDER THE STARS AND STRIPES.

The Buzzard to the Vultures—Well, Fellows, We Might as Well Pull Out. If We Stay Here We'll Starve—Uncle Sam Is Running Things Here From Now On, and Our Business Is Ruined.—July 20

---

once introduced into the city of Santiago under United States management, and it seemed the vultures and buzzards who had so long thrived under Spanish misrule would be out of a job. It

WAITING FOR WATSON'S GREATEST SHOW ON EARTH.
July 22

was reported in the papers on July 21, under a Gibraltar date line, that warships of foreign powers were cruising in the vicinity of the expected naval conflict to come off when Watson arrived. • The French fleet was there and certain Italian warships, presumably to see the show. Bull fight-

TOO MUCH REAL FIGHTING FOR THEM.

Spanish Bull Fighter—Yes, Bull Fights Have Been Stopped During The War.
American Prize Fighter—And You Can't Get Anyone to Listen to Prize Fight Talk Now-a-Days.
Both—This War Is Wrong for Sure.—July 25.

---

ing was suspended in Spain, and as for the American prize-fighter he could not get in a word edgewise. This play fighting was tame in those warlike days, and the gentlemen of these professions

THE CIGARETTE OF PEACE.

Alphonso—Here, Old Man, Smoke One of These with Me. July 27.

---

were made to condole together. President McKinley, on July 26, received a note from the Spanish cabinet asking for an armistice, and the little King asked Uncle Sam to have a sweet peace cigarette

SAFE!

July 2.

with him. The peace proposal ball which followed immediately did not reach the baseman until Gen. Miles was safe at Porto Rico, and so could not be deprived of holding that base for Uncle

WHAT WILL HATCH OUT OF IT?

July 29.

Sam. And now that the peace proposal egg was under the American eagle, Spain was much concerned as to what would be hatched from it. It was decided that Porto Rico was to have a new

SOMETHING LACKING.

Uncle Sam—Well Sonny, What Is It?
Phil Ippines—Where Do I Come In on This? —July 30

suit of Stars and Stripes and Cuba to have his long desired free Cuba flag, but according to the plans then talked most the poor little Philippine savage was to be abandoned without anything.

EVEN UNCLE PLATT RECOGNIZES THE EFFECTIVENESS OF A ROUGH RIDER.

August 2.

Politics and war were doomed to blend all over the country this year, and even Uncle Platt recognized the effectiveness of a rough rider when Teddy Roosevelt, all fresh from the war, put the G. O. P. through a few paces on the New York political track. While the Peace Protocol was not

THE WAR EAGLE AND THE DOVES OF PEACE.

The American War Eagle—Well, I've Had My Day and I Suppose It's Time to Give These Pretty Things a Show.—August 5.

signed until August 12, on August 6 it was understood Spain would accept the peace terms offered by the United States. For some days prior to this date the war eagle had yielded his place of honor to the doves of peace and interest was centered about the peace negotiations at Washington where

"THEY'RE ALL RIGHT."

The G. O. P.—These Durn Newspapers Say that Uncle Sam Has a White Elephant on His Hands in the Philippines—Well! What's The Matter With Elephants?—August 6.

the French minister was representing Spain. Public opinion had taken a flop on the Philippine question and people were beginning to realize that the United States must retain these islands which Dewey had placed in our possession. A good deal had been said in the papers about the Philippines being an elephant on our hands and the G.O.P. took the stand indicated—Well: what's

WHAT SPLENDID USE WE COULD HAVE MADE OF THE GRANDFATHER'S HAT.

August 8.

the matter with elephants? As soon as Spain agreed to the terms of peace, President McKinley began to look around for peace commissioners and the great head that is in Grandfather Ben Harrison's hat was one of the first chosen. The fact that he declined the honor the day the cartoon of August 8 was published was no reason for leaving out of print what would have been so

IN TIMES OF WAR PREPARE FOR PEACE.

Uncle Sam Can Beat Spain at this Kind of Game, Too. Only Let Him Get His Talking Force Together.—August 9.

fitting a cartoon had he accepted. Uncle Sam had whipped Spain badly in the fighting game and now that the talking game was to begin there was no reason why, with the force of talkers Uncle Sam always has on hand, that he should not whip the Latin race worse in the game of talk. It

THE EXPANSION POLICY.

G. O. P. to D. D.—Better Pitch In Old Fellow and Get an Expansion on Yourself.—August 11.

was no even contest for Spain. The two parties seated at the table spread with the luxuries of new domain had the choice, of eating or not eating, as a policy. The G. O. P. at once decided to eat. The democratic party, as a party, seemed inclined to sit back and let the good things alone. Poor fellow, he is likely to go hungry a long time in consequence of this anti-expansion policy. On

SIGNS OF PEACE.

August 12.

August 12 came substantial "Signs of Peace." M. Jules Cambon, the French minister, affixed his signature to the peace protocol, representing Spain, and Secretary of State Day signed for the

THEY SPEAK FROM EXPERIENCE.
The Eagle—Don't You Fellows Get to Scrapping Now. War's a Bad Thing at the Best.
The Vulture—An' When You Get the Worst of It—But Don't Ask for Particulars. August 13.

United States. The American Eagle and the Vulture of Spain had no sooner perched themselves on the wall of the war arena to talk up peace than growls from the Russian Bear and the English Lion indicated we might have another bout in the arena. Perhaps the advice of the birds

CAN'T ALL GO HOME.

August 17

served to warn them. The fighting done, the volunteers were released from the service as rapidly as possible but the gunner who took up the battle weeks before they went into the field still had to stand by his gun of diplomacy. Surely the United States had good reason to be proud of the man

OVERHEARD IN THE NATIONAL ART GALLERY.

Porto Rico—I Reckon He Must Be our Step-Father—Eh, Hawaii?

---

behind the gun. A great deal of speculation was indulged in as to what George Washington would think of the country adopting these island peoples. Porto Rico and Hawaii may have done a little figuring too as to their relation to the Father of His Country. Admiral Sampson as head of the

SAMPSON TAKES HAVANA.

Captain General Blanco—This Is Better Than the Pipe of Peace and Answers the Same Purpose.—August 19.

evacuation commission went to Cuba on the Flagship New York with other members of the commission and the Fifth regular infantry to look after American interests in Cuba while the Spanish were moving out. In far away Manilla, Dewey kept right on fighting on his own hook. While the

THERE AIN'T GOIN' TO BE NO CORE.

August 20.

---

signatures were being affixed to the peace protocol Manilla was falling. By the time official news of the peace arrangements had reached Dewey he had good possession of the Philippine apple and it was apparent there "wasn't goin' to be no core" for little Alphonso. The war spirit had long

QUELLING THE INDIAN OUTBREAK.

August '22.

---

been kindled in the youth of the land. It only needed Buffalo Bill's Wild West show with his real Cubans and Indians and all kinds of soldiers to come to town to fan it into a flame. Then we had real war right in our midst and it took the strong hand of authority to quell it. The terms of

WHAT "SUBURBS" MEANS TO UNOLE SAM.

August 13.

peace gave Uncle Sam possession of Manilla and its suburbs. Of course after building a Greater New York and a Chicago, Uncle Sam's definition of suburbs easily stretched over the entire Philip-

A VALUABLE ADDITION TO THE REPAST.

Jamaica-Ginger—Uncle Sam, I Thought You Would be Likely to Want Me After Absorbing All That Green Fruit.—August 21

pine group. The people of Jamaica could see the advantages to be derived by Cuba and Porto Rico under the protection of the United States and they talked very freely of offering themselves to Uncle Sam to go along with the tropical fruit he was assimilating. We could not all go to war to

LICKING THE WAR REVENUE STAMPS.

Uncle Sam—It Took Me Three Months to Lick Spain, but There's No Telling How Long it will Take Me to Lick These Stamps.—August 28.

help lick Spain, but we all had a chance to bear our share by licking the war revenue stamps and

MILES--SHOOT IF YOU DARE.

August 27.

this was a good deal the longer process. When Alger began putting charges in that court martial gun for General Miles the General smiled at the old blunderbuss and thought how the old thing would kick the Secretary of War. Perhaps Alger thought of this too, as he never pulled the trigger.

UNCLE SAM HOBSONIZED.

Our Lady of Snows Salutes Heroism in Her Neighbor on His Return From the War.—August 2[illegible].

Canada as well as England gave Uncle Sam cordial support during the unpleasantness with Spain and was outspoken in her friendliness. One of the good jokes following the war was the

THAT PROPOSED DISARMAMENT.

The Bear—Say, Fellows, Let's All Pull Our Teeth So We Can't Fight.
The Others—All Right, but What's the Matter With Pulling Out Yours First? August 30.

Czar's proposed disarmament. The other animals to whom the Bear proposed the joke all enjoyed it immensely and then the Bear grew a full set of new teeth. Hard times got killed some time

HIS TURN NOW.

Mr. Factory Chimney to Thirteen Inch Gun—Well, I Guess You're Through. Now, Just Watch My Smoke.—August 31.

during the war. People quit talking of him during the exciting times and he may have died a natural death or perhaps was struck by a stray shell. Any way when the thirteen-inch gun quit smoking the factory chimney was ready to begin in good earnest. The country spent weeks after

TOO MUCH FOR HIM.

The Spanish Devil Fish Was Easy for the American Soldier, but the Official Red Tape Worm of the War Department Is a More Voracious Beast.—September 1.

---

the war was over fixing the blame. It was not far to find and most every one will agree that it was the red tape worm. The army life was undoubtedly hard on our volunteers and many returned

THE WANDERER'S RETURN.

Joe Klon Dike—Hello, old man! Didn't know you had been over the trail; you're thinner'n a match.
Will Volunteer—The Klondike's not the only anti-fat. I've been in camp for Uncle Sam.—September 5.

---

from the camps weak and sick from the experience. The returning gold hunter had good reason to recognize the Klondike face on Will Volunteer. Uncle Sam got himself into a big job of

BREAKING NEW GROUND.

Uncle Sam, Having Put His Hand to the Plow Cannot Turn Back.—September 8.

plowing when he started out with the team of Justice and Humanity. He broke new ground for Cuba and would gladly have not entered the Philippine field, but once in it with his hand to the plow he could not turn back. What will the harvest be? Joseph Chamberlain, of England, came

UNCLE SAM SEEMS TO UNDERSTAND ENGLISH.

Joseph Chamberlain of England—"I Say, Old Man, Colonization Is Always a Good Thing for Any Country, Don't 'Cher Know?"—September 7.

to make Uncle Sam a visit and he was just full of advice about colonization. He was interviewed by the newspapers and wrote articles for the magazines and the funny part of it was that Uncle

PEACE SHOULD BEGIN AT HOME.

Uncle Sam—Guess I'd Better Use That Peace Commission at Home Before I Send It Abroad. September 10

Sam could understand his English perfectly. This was something new. A year before and it would have been all Greek to Uncle. Uncle Sam could have used that peace commission at home to good advantage to settle the difficulty between Alger and Miles. It was one of the most bitter engagements of the war. In the Philippines Aguinaldo had an uncomfortable way of collecting

IT MAKES A DIFFERENCE.

Uncle Sam to Little Aguinaldo—See Here Sonny, Whom Are You Going to Throw Those Rocks At?—September 12.

ammunition and storing up firearms. These he said were to be used on Spain but Uncle Sam got an idea some way that they might be used on himself and Aguinaldo was watched. When Teddy

THE REAL BRONCO BUSTER.

Teddy Roosevelt Seems to Stick Pretty Tight to His Political Mount.—September 14

Roosevelt's Rough Riders had to leave him they presented him with Remington's statue of the Bronco Buster. This called out several cartoons for and against the dauntless colonel. On the

HIS POLICY.

Johnny (Home Again) Expansion? You Bet, Mother! I Believe in Expansion, to the Limit. September 19.

same day as the Minneapolis Journal published its Bronco Buster cartoon, Davenport, of the New York Journal, published one on the same subject but he made Teddy the horse and Platt the rider. Poor fellow he was working for an off side paper and had to do the best he could with a good subject. When Johnny came marching home from the camps of beans and hardtack and bacon to his mother's well laden table, you may depend upon it, his policy was expansion to the limit. Ger-

A PERTINENT QUESTION.

Uncle Sam—Well, What Is It to You, My German Friend, Whether There Is Coal Here or Not?—September 30.

many had the nerve to take a coal hod and go poking around over on one of our Philippine islands and actually reported a find of coal there. But that was all the good it ever did Germany.

A PARTY WITHOUT AN ISSUE IN ITS SEARCH FOR ONE.

I do not speak now of that other item which certain newspapers and others are trying to make the leading issue of the democratic campaign. Forgetting the glory, the achievement, the success with which an army of 200,000 men was raised out of nothing and a hostile nation almost wiped out in ninety days, they are hovering like buzzards over the battlefields and hospitals and graveyards, looking only for the misery and suffering and death which are inevitable in war. Surely the democratic party has not been reduced so low in the supply of proper subjects for political division as to seem to rely upon yellow fever and yellow literature.—United States Attorney General Griggs before the New Jersey Republicans.—Sept. 21.

ON THE BACK TRACK.

Christopher Columbus—Now I Suppose I Have Got to Go Back and Discover These Spaniards.—September 28

Columbus' bones were unearthed from their resting place in Havana before Blanco left, and the discoverer was sent back to see if poor old Spain were still on earth. He did not find her the proud nation which so cruelly mistreated him a few centuries ago. When Augustus Van Wyck

THE ROUGH RIDING BEGINS IN NEW YORK.

September 30.

mounted the Tammany Tiger the Rough Riding began in New York. Had it not been for Teddy Roosevelt's experience in this line and his new but glorious record as a fighter, the race might have

The Old Pupil Turns out to Be the Worst One in the Class.--October 7.

come out otherwise. The Indian outbreak in Minnesota showed that as a fighter Uncle Sam still had a worse ward in the Indian than in any of the new pupils he had just taken into his school to

UNCLE SAM AS THE CRUEL LANDLORD.

October 8.

train in the ways of civilization. The Spaniards showed a disposition to linger in Cuba, and Porto Rico and Uncle Sam found it necessary to play the part of the cruel landlord. On October 7, he posted notices of eviction in both houses. It was left for the governor of Minnesota to give the

A ROAST FOR THE WAR DEPARTMENT.

Old-Man-Not-Afraid-of-Red-Tape gets his war paint on and warms up the war department at Washington.—October 10.

war department a roast that really counted. The war department procrastinated to its heart's content about sending supplies and men to Cuba, but when they dallied over long in sending men to put down the Indians, Old-Man-Not-Afraid-Of-Red-Tape put on his war paint and sent the go-to-

OUR HERO GOVERNOR SAFE.

Lieutenant Hobson - Great scheme that, governor; let me congratulate you. Too bad I didn't think of it, but I was taken unawares, you know.—October 12.

the-devil telegram, and proceeded to raise men for himself. This made a hero of governor Clough. New York papers ran his picture and displayed his deed in big type head lines. But hero's were

TRAVELED MILES TO LEARN.

Big Chief Sat-On-By-The-Fat-Man—How! How! Sat on the q. t., Dave, how did you do it?
Big Chief Not-Afraid-of-Red-Tape—Ugh! Ugh! It was easy.—October 15.

not safe from the kisses of the ladies in war times, as Hobson and others found. The Governor's protection was pictured for Journal readers. Big Chief Miles came this way and stopped at the wigwam of the Chief Not-Afraid-Of-Red-Tape, to find how the governor had succeeded in doing

HOUSE CLEANING AT THE WHITE HOUSE.

The House Cleaner—First chance I've had to clean up since Mac came here. That man works too much. Now, when Grover was here the ducks were flying and the fish biting frequently.—October 17.

what he had tried to do during the entire war. When President McKinley came west to the Omaha Exposition and the Chicago peace jubilee, the people who take care of the executive mansion had their first chance to give it a thorough overhauling. This was the President's first relief from work since the Maine sailed to Havana. Much of the time he had actually worked night and day.

SURPRISED HIM.

Spain—McKinley Made a Doctor! Why, I Thought He was a Doctor already. Here I've Been Taking His Medicine in Big Doses for Five Months or more.- October 18

When President McKinley reached Chicago he was voted a degree by the Chicago University and made, with much ceremony, Dr. McKinley. And Spain had been taking his medicine thinking he was a Doctor all the time. Lieut. Hobson proved himself well trained in engineering as well as

ONE THING HOBSON COULDN'T RAISE.

Spain—I Insist That You Take This, Too.
Hobson—Don't You Do It, Uncle Sam. It Will Take More Than Wind Bags to Raise It.—October 19.

---

in bravery. His work in raising the Spanish battle ships, sunk at Santiago, gained for him the reputation of being ready to raise anything. He did raise the mortgage on his old home in Alabama, but he saw no hopes of raising the Cuban debt which was at the time the issue before the peace commission. A valuable shipment started from Minneapolis to Manilla just previous to

NEW JOB FOR "OLD SANTY."

He Has One Errand Where "Dancer," "Prancer," "Comet" and "Vixen" Are Not Available.—October 21.

Oct. 24. It was the offering of Minnesota friends to the soldier boys in Manilla. Santa Claus had to go into the expansion business in earnest. A year made a great deal of difference with Uncle Sam's

THEIR FIRST THANKSGIVING.

Uncle Sam—Hawaii, Will You Have Some of the White Meat?

family. No one would have dreamed a year before that when the President issued his thanksgiving proclamation for 1898 it would call so many little island urchins to table to be thankful for being under his protection. The American peace commission, during the last of October, broke it gently

THE YANKEE PIG AGAIN.

American Peace Commission —"Whole Hog or None" Is the American Idea and In Regard to the Philippines It's — Whole Hog.— November 1.

to Spain that we must have all of the Philippine group. We would put up the cash, but we must have— if it pleased the Spanish people to look at it that way— the whole hog.

AN INTERESTED SPECTATOR.

Is It Worth While to Give the Administration Your Vote of Confidence at This Time, or Not?—November 3.

The Washington dispatches yesterday said: "Spain hopes to delay the presentation of the second proposition until the following Monday and by the time of the next sitting the elections in the United States will have taken place, and if they should show opposition to the policy of the administration the Spaniards will maintain a firmer stand against the demands of the American commissioners with some hope of securing material modifications. Advices received from Mr. Day for several weeks have shown that the Spanish commissioners have been building great hope of the defeat of the republican party during the coming election."

A SLIGHT INTERRUPTION.

Uncle Sam—Excuse Me a Minute Until I Look Over These Returns.—November 8.

On Nov. 8, Uncle Sam had to interrupt his discussions with Spain long enough to look at the

WITH THE POLITIOAL ROUGH RIDERS.

President McKinley Takes an Endorsement Ride With His Friends on the G. O. P. November 9.

election returns. These returns showed that the country endorsed the President in his policy of

NO LONGER A GAME OF CHANCE.

Prest. McKinley Now Holds a Winning Hand.—November 11.

expansion. This election deal left president McKinley with a sure winning hand in the future, and the Spanish player had nothing to gain by delay. The game was soon up. Blanco took flight from Cuba

FIGHTING "GROVE" TO THE FRONT.

Blanco—About Time We Were Getting Out of Here. Grover Always Goes Home With a Full Bag. November 19.

early in November to escape the sight of the American troops marching into Havana. Or was it because "Fighting Grove" was headed for Cuba in search of game. Uncle Sam paid $20,000,000 to

A STOCKING FROM UNCLE SAMTA CLAUS.

Little Alphonso—Well, the Old Fellow Really Wasn't So Bad After All.—November 29.

Spain for the Philippine islands, and after all the talk of yielding to force, this must have seemed to the poor little king like quite a snug Christmas stocking from his Uncle Samta Claus.

NEW WEIGHT IN THE BALANCE EUROPEAN VIEW OF IT.

November 30.

FLAGGING THE TRAIN OF PROGRESS.

Somebody's Got to Get Off the Track.—December 1.

Before the Senate met it was pretty well understood who would make up the obstruction crew to stop, if possible, President McKinley's train of progress. There were those who showed a dispo-

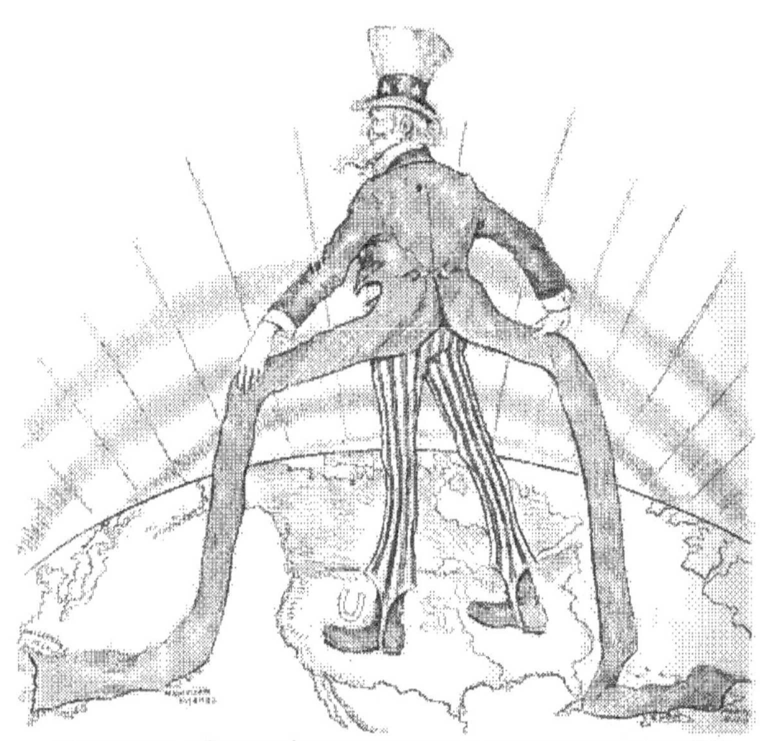

UNCLE SAM - DID ANYONE SAY HE WISHED TO TREAD ON THE TAILS OF MY COAT?

December 3.

sition to tread on the tails of Uncle Sam's coat when he spread them out in the Orient. Germany, in particular, was not polite, but he decided not to walk on our coat tails. When the House and

THE OPENING OF CONGRESS.

Well, Boys, Get Busy—There's Work For You.—December 5.

Senate returned from their vacation, the East was snow bound ; but the beautiful snow of national business, which had accumulated in drifts about the National Capitol, was a snow fall without a

THIS SOLVES THE CUBAN PROBLEM.

Give the Youth of Cuba an American College Education and in the Future They Will Defend Themselves Against Any Foreign Oppressor.—December 8.

parallel in the memory of the oldest inhabitant. A movement was at once started in the United States to give deserving Cuban youths American college educations, the only requirement being

THE "OPEN DOOR" POLICY.
Some People Find It Rather Chilly.—December 10.

that the young men return to their native land. Leading colleges opened their doors, and prominent men were named to receive funds from those who wished to contribute to the cause. New England furnished more than her share of the growlers around the stove in the country

FORGIVE AND FORGET.

Uncle Sam—Well, Old Man, I've Licked You Good and Plenty. I hated to Do It, but I Had to. All the Same, I Ain't a Harborin' of No Grudges, and If it's Agreeable to You We'll Be Friends Again. Eh?—December 12.

---

store who grumbled at President McKinley's Open Door Policy. The dates Jan. 26—Dec. 10 include the war in its entirety. The good ship Maine sailed for Havana on the first date; the Peace

SOMETHING IN COMMON AT LAST.

December [illegible]

Treaty was signed on the last, and the cartoons within this cover with one exception cover that period. Strange, wasn't it, that these two ship wrecked mariners, never before able to agree on anything, should drift about on the political sea and at last find themselves hanging to the same plank.

Chronology of the War.

1898.

Jan. 24—Battleship Maine ordered to Havana on a peaceful mission.

Feb. 10—De Lome, Spanish minister, recalled for unwarranted personalities reflecting on President McKinley.

Feb. 15—Battleship Maine blown up in Havana harbor; 266 lives lost.

Feb. 17—United States board of inquiry on the loss of the Maine appointed.

Feb. 20—Spanish cruiser Viscaya anchors off Staten Island, N. Y.

Feb. 22—Spanish board of inquiry reports destruction of the Maine an accident of internal origin.

March 9—Emergency bill, $50,000,000, for United States defenses, passed.

March 28—The president sends Maine report to congress.

April 9—General Lee and other consuls leave Cuba.

April 11—The president sends a message to congress recommending armed intervention in Cuba.

April 16—Intervention resolutions passed by the Senate.

April 19—House passes intervention resolutions.

April 19—The president prepares an ultimatum to Spain demanding evacuation of Cuba within three days.

April 20—Cuban resolutions signed by the president.

April 20—Spanish minister, Polo y Bernabe, asks for his passports.

April 21—United States minister, General Woodford, given his passports in Madrid.

April 21—Spain's severance of diplomatic relations held to be a declaration of war.

April 22—North Atlantic squadron sails to blockade Cuban ports.

April 22—First shot fired when United States gunboat Nashville captured Spanish coast trader Buena Ventura.

April 23—The president's call issued for 125,000 volunteers.

April 24—Spain's first shot at United States from masked batteries at Matanzas on United States gunboat Foote.

April 27—Asiatic squadron sails from Hongkong to meet the Spanish fleet at the Philippine Islands.

April 27—Batteries at Matanzas bombarded.

April 29—Batteries at Cienfuegos bombarded.

April 30—Batteries at Cabanas bombarded.

May 1—Spanish fleet at Manilla destroyed by Commodore Dewey.

May 5—Sampson's fleet leaves Key West for Porto Rico.

May 6—Pope advises queen regent to appeal to powers.

May 6—Minnesota regiments mustered in.

May 9—Fight at Cardenas between Winslow and three Spanish gunboats, Ensign Bagley and four men killed.

May 10—Dewey nominated Rear Admiral by the President.

May 11—Cable off Cienfuegos cut.

May 12—San Juan, Porto Rico, bombarded.

May 12—George Downing, Spanish spy, commits suicide in Washington.

May 14—Cape Verde fleet off Martinique.

May 16—12th and 14th Minn. leave for Chickamauga, 13th for San Francisco.

May 18—Charleston sails for Manilla. First reinforcement for Dewey.

May 24—Cape Verde fleet announced at Santiago.

May 25—Oregon arrives at Jupiter Inlet, Fla.

May 25—President issues second call for 75,000 volunteers.

May 27—Schley arrives at Santiago.

May 28—Santiago blockade begun.

May 30—Troops embark at Tampa.

May 31—Santiago forts bombarded.

June 3—Hobson sinks the Merrimac.

June 6—Bombardment of Santiago forts.

June 7—Monterey sails for Manilla.

June 11—Fight at Guantanamo, 2 marines killed.

June 13—Shafter sails for Cuba.

June 20—Shafter's army arrives at Baiquiri.

June 21—Charleston seizes the Ladrones.

June 22 and 23—Shafter's army lands.

June 23—Juragua captured.

June 24—Fight at La Quasina.

June 26—Cadiz fleet at Port Said.

June 26—Shafter occupies Sevilla.

June 27—13th Minn. sails for Manilla.

June 30—El Caney evacuated by the Spaniards.

July 1—Outer defenses of Santiago taken.

July 2—San Juan, near Santiago, taken.

July 3—Shafter demands surrender of Santiago.

July 3—Cervera's fleet destroyed.

July 4—Call issued for 15th Minn.

July 6—McKinley issues thanksgiving proclamation.

July 7—Hobson and men exchanged.

July 10—Bombardment of Santiago resumed; Linares refuses unconditional surrender.

July 10—Bombardment continued and investment completed.

July 12—Miles arrives at Santiago.

July 13—Truce.

July 14—Santiago surrenders.

July 17—Stars and Stripes hoisted at Santiago.

July 18—15th Minn. mustered in at Camp Ramsey.

July 21—Miles sails from Guantanamo with 18,000 troops for Porto Rico.

July 25—Gen. Miles' advance lands at Guanica, Porto Rico.

July 26—M. Cambon, French Ambassador, proposes peace.

July 27—Ponce, Porto Rico, surrenders.

July 30—Answer to Spain's peace overture delivered to Cambon.

July 31—13th Minn. arrives at Manilla.

Aug. 10—Peace protocol agreed to by Spain.

Aug. 11—Hostilities cease.

Aug. 12—Peace protocol signed.

Aug. 13—Manilla surrenders.

Aug. 15—Merritt declares martial law in Manilla.

Aug. 16—Cuban and Porto Rican evacuation committee appointed.

Aug. 20—Repatriation of Spanish soldiers begins.

Aug. 20—Aguinaldo accepts American terms.

Aug. 27—Col. Reeve breveted Brigadier General.

Sep. 3—12th and 14th Minn. ordered mustered out.

Sep. 10—War investigation commission appointed.

Sep. 15—15th Minn. leaves Ft. Snelling for Camp Meade, Pa.

Sep. 17—12th Minn. arrives St. Paul.

Sep. 17—Spanish peace commission appointed.

Sept. 17—U. S. peace commission sails from New York.

Sep. 23—14th Minn. arrives at St. Paul.

Sep. 24—First meeting of the war investigation commission.

Sep. 27—American peace commission arrives Paris.

Oct. 3—Merritt arrives Paris from Manilla.

Oct. 18—Porto Rico formally occupied.

Nov. 1—Maria Teresa abandoned while being brought to United States.

Nov. 15—15th Minn. leaves Camp Meade for Monte Sano Heights, Ga.

Nov. 21—American commission ultimatum offering $20,000,000 for Philippines.

Nov. 25—American troops arrive at Havana.

Nov. 28—Spanish commission agrees to accept American offer for Philippines.

Dec. 10—Peace Treaty signed.

www.ingramcontent.com/pod-product-compliance
Lightning Source LLC
Chambersburg PA
CBHW021114020726
47500CB00003B/745

* 9 7 8 3 7 4 1 1 9 1 5 9 6 *